POCKET
BEARS

Methuen/Moonlight
First Published in Great Britain 1979
by Blackie & Son Ltd
Copyright © 1979 Annette Betz Verlag
First published 1983 in Pocket Bears by
Methuen Children's Books Ltd, 11 New Fetter
Lane, London EC4 in association with
Moonlight Publishing Ltd, 131 Kensington
Church Street, London W8

Printed in Italy by La Editoriale Libraria

ISBN 0 907144 31 4

PETER AND THE WOLF

told by Sergei Prokofiev
illustrated by Erna Voigt

methuen ☾ moonlight

We hope that you will enjoy the story and illustrations in this book, but there is more to 'Peter and the Wolf' than words and pictures. The music which Sergei Prokofiev composed for this story has made it the most popular musical tale ever written for children.

Violin

Each character in the story is introduced by one of the instruments of the orchestra. Here they all are: Peter with the violin, Grandfather with the bassoon, the duck with the oboe, the cat with the clarinet and the wolf with the French horn. The hunters go rat-tat on the kettle drum and the little bird trills on the flute.

One morning, Peter opened the garden gate...

and walked out into the great, green meadow. Sitting in a tree was Peter's friend, the little bird.

Flute

"All is quiet. All is well,"
chirped the bird happily as
Peter came to meet him.

Behind Peter waddled the duck. She was glad to see that Peter had not shut the gate, for now she could go and swim in the clear, blue pond which lay in the middle of the meadow. When the little bird saw the duck swimming in the pond, he flew over and began to tease her.

Oboe

"Call yourself a bird, when you can't even fly!" he taunted. "Call yourself a bird, when you can't even swim!" quacked the duck, flapping her wings in annoyance.

They were so busy quarrelling that neither of them noticed the cat slinking through the bushes. The cat was thinking, ''While they are arguing I shall creep up on that bird and catch him!''

Clarinet

Suddenly Peter saw the cat.
"Look out!" he shouted. The
bird swooped up into the tree
and the duck retreated to the
middle of the pond and quacked
crossly at the cat.

Just then Grandfather came out of the house. He was angry with Peter for leaving the garden gate open and going into the meadow alone.
"The meadow is a dangerous place," he said.

Bassoon

"What would you have done if a wolf had come out of the forest?" He took Peter back into the garden and closed the gate firmly.

No sooner had Peter left the meadow than a large grey wolf did come creeping out of the forest.

French Horn

The cat ran quickly up into a tree.

The duck squawked nervously and came rushing out of the pond.

Oboe

The wolf saw her and began to chase her. How ever fast the poor duck ran he came nearer and nearer and then snapped her up and swallowed her!

Then the wolf peered up into the tree, where the cat was sitting on one branch, and the bird on another—not too close.

Violin

The wolf paced around the tree, staring hungrily at them. Meanwhile, Peter, who had seen everything and was not at all frightened of the wolf, had run into the house to fetch some rope.

Peter climbed onto a branch of the tree, saying to the little bird, "Flutter round the wolf's nose— but don't let him catch you!"

Flute

The little bird fluttered and flapped, and try as he might the wolf could not catch him.

Peter made a loop at the end of his rope and lowered it carefully over the wolf's tail. The he pulled the loop tight and the wolf was trapped!

Violin

The wolf began to leap about, trying to free himself, but Peter had tied the other end of the rope to the tree, and the wolf's struggles only pulled the loop tighter.

Just then three hunters came through the forest, firing their guns. They were following the trail of the wolf.

Kettle Drum

"Look, he went this way!" they cried, and fired their guns again—
bang! bang! bang!

But Peter called down from his tree, ''Why are you shooting?

Kettle Drum

The little bird and I have already
caught the wolf!''

So they all set off in a triumphant procession to take the wolf to the zoo. Peter led the way, followed by the hunters. Then came Grandfather, shaking his head and muttering, "Suppose Peter had not caught the wolf? What would have happened then?"

Oboe

The little bird flew overhead
chirping merrily, and if you
listened very carefully you could
hear the duck quacking inside
the wolf's stomach. In his greed
the wolf had swallowed her
whole, and she was still alive!